In memory of H. B. Thomas—
one of His best and most beautiful dreamers
—C.R.

And for Eliza Louise Harper
—B.M.

THE

Cynthia Rylant

DREAMER

Illustrated by Barry Moser

THE BLUE SKY PRESS

An Imprint of Scholastic Inc. • *New York*

The Blue Sky Press

For information regarding permission,
please write to:
    Permissions Department,
    The Blue Sky Press,
    an imprint of Scholastic Inc.,
    730 Broadway, New York, New York 10003

The Blue Sky Press is a trademark of Scholastic Inc.

Library of Congress Cataloging-in-Publication Data
Rylant, Cynthia
The dreamer / Cynthia Rylant; illustrated by Barry Moser.
    p.   cm.
    Summary: From his dreams an artist creates the earth, sky,
trees, and all the creatures that dwell on our planet.
        ISBN 0-590-47341-7
        [1. Artists—Fiction. 2. Creation—Fiction. 3. Dreams—Fiction.]
I. Moser, Barry, ill. II. Title.
PZ7.R982Dr   1993
[E]—dc20   93-19915
CIP
12 11 10 9 8 7 6 5 4 3 2 1   3 4 5 6 7 8/9
Printed in the United States of America   36
First printing, October 1993

THE DREAMER

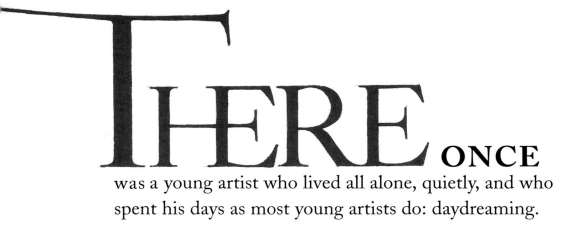

T HERE ONCE was a young artist who lived all alone, quietly, and who spent his days as most young artists do: daydreaming.

It was a lovely way of living. He would simply lie about, thinking, wondering, perhaps making small wishes. And as he dreamed in his mind, he would see something he hadn't seen before. Something beautiful. Something new.

Then one day—as often happens with young artists— he decided he would make what he saw in his mind.

So he made a star. He was surprised at how well it turned out, and shyly pleased with himself, and having so well made this one thing, he was inspired to make more.

So—as often happens with young artists—he worked all night long making stars and by morning he was surrounded by heavens.

His heavens twinkled and shone, and standing in this radiant beauty, the young artist was inspired to daydream again. He rested among the stars until he found something new in his mind. He set about making this new thing. He worked all night long.

By morning he had made an earth. Round and sturdy, full of bumps and chunks and ridges. It borrowed the light of the heavens and sat full of form and grace. The young artist, shyly pleased with himself, rested his back against a smooth ridge and gently closed his eyes.

And after a time, he saw another thing in his mind:

Blue water. This he painted onto the hard, dry earth, giving it color. The young artist loved the color and wanted more. So he floated on the blue water and dreamed. In time he saw this:

Green grass. He painted soft, sweet-smelling green grass and—
as young artists will almost always do—he got carried away and
painted some trees.

He painted green grass and trees all night long and by morning he was in a forest, sleepy, and he lay down under a giant pine to dream. In his dreams he saw many, many new things and they all moved like life.

When he woke up, he made every living thing he had seen in his mind and when he was finished, the whales parted the blue seas, the birds dotted the green trees, and a cow nuzzled his hand.

He moved among these living creatures and—like all young artists—felt such joy and love for his creation that he thought he might explode with happiness. He wanted to tell *someone* what he had done, to show *someone* his beautiful heavens and earth and water and grass and moving creatures, and he looked all around him but the world was empty of anyone who might listen and understand. Someone with ears to hear and eyes to see. Someone who was an artist as well.

So he worked all night long. And by morning he had made a
new artist in his own image. Shyly pleased with himself, he
made another one. He loved the company. He made one more.

The world began filling up with artists. These made new ones and the new ones made even newer ones and, of course, they all loved to daydream. Living among blue water and green grass, they have daydreamed the most beautiful things in the world.

The first young artist, still a dreamer, has always called them
his children.

And they, in turn, have always called him God.

The illustrations in this book were executed with watercolor
on paper handmade by Simon Green for Barcham Green
in Maidstone, Kent, Great Britain, especially for the Royal Watercolor Society.

The text type was set in Adobe Caslon by WLCR.

The display type was set in Caslon 540 by American Type Founders Co., Inc.

The calligraphy was done by Reassurance Wunder, North Hatfield, Massachusetts.

Color separations were made by Color Dot Graphics, Inc.

Printed and bound by Horowitz/Rae

Typographic direction by Claire B. Counihan

Production supervision by Angela Biola

Designed by Barry Moser